YOU ARE WONDERFUL

A UNIQUE COLLECTION OF SHORT STORIES FOR GIRLS AND BOYS ABOUT LOVE, GRATITUDE AND STRENGTH

KATHERINE LINDGREEN

ISBN – 9798839887886

THIS BOOK BELONGS TO

_____

TABLE OF CONTENTS

Story #1: Cream's New Friend 1

Story #2: Swan Pond 7

Story #3: Princess Nina 13

Story #4: The Making of Pearls 18

Story #5- Lightning Bug Cove 25

Story #6- Anna's Garden...32

Story #7- Thunder to the Rescue 39

Story #8- A Tale of Two Princes...45

Story #9- Maria and the Wolves..51

Story #10- Lola's Drawings 58

Disclaimer...63

STORY #1: CREAM'S NEW FRIEND

Cream was a happy kitten. Every morning, she would wake up in a patch of sunlight, eat her breakfast of milk and tuna, then head out into the forest to play with her three best friends: Dot, Rusty, and Smoky.

Dot lived in the house next to Cream's with her human, and Rusty and Smoky were brothers who lived across the street. The happy foursome spent their days frolicking through the woods, climbing trees, and lapping up the water dripping off moss-covered rocks.

One morning, Cream woke up especially excited. Today, she and her friends had made big plans to climb to the very top of the tallest pine tree in the forest. Although she would not admit it, Cream was a little bit scared. You could barely even see the top of the tree from the ground, and it would put her as high up as the birds flying!

But Cream's excitement was bigger than her fear, so she happily ate her breakfast and tore out the back door to find her three friends. She jumped onto the fence, looking into the woods for the other kittens. She could just barely make out their huddled shapes, already waiting for her under the pine tree.

Just as she was getting ready to jump down, she heard a voice from behind her.

"Hello! I just moved in. My name is Ember. Would you like to play?"

Cream turned around to face a kitten she had never seen before. White and orange, this kitten was staring at her eagerly, her tail tucked expectantly over her paws.

"I just moved in over there." Ember flicked her nose at the house on the other side of Cream's. "Would you like to play with me in the woods?"

Cream hesitated. She had never had any other friends beside Dot, Smoky, and Rusty. What if this kitten didn't fit in?

"I'm a little busy today," Cream said. "Maybe tomorrow?"

Ember's eyes dimmed a little bit, but she nodded. "Okay."

With that, Cream hopped off of the fence and raced towards the woods to meet up with her friends. They all sat at the bottom of the tree, arguing who would be the one to climb first. They argued for so long it got dark, and they had to return home for bedtime.

"We'll try again tomorrow," Dot promised.

The next morning, they all met under the tree once again. As they began their discussion of who would go first, they heard the footsteps of another cat approaching.

It was Ember again. "Hello!" Ember said cheerfully. "I'm Ember. Would you guys like to play with me?"

All four kittens stared at Ember without speaking. Like Cream, they had never had any other friends aside from each other. And like Cream, they were all thinking the same thing: what if Ember didn't fit in with them?

Dot spoke first. "Sorry, Ember. We're busy today. We're trying to climb that tree. Maybe another time."

This time, Ember looked sad. "Oh," she said softly, turning to walk away. "Okay." She walked away, her head down and her tail drooping.

Cream watched Ember go and couldn't help but feel a little bad. She imagined how sad she would feel if she didn't have any friends to play with. *It must be lonely*, she thought.

The kittens spent another full day arguing over who would climb the tree.

"Someone has to go first tomorrow!" Smoky finally declared, as the sun was setting over the trees. The four kittens made a pact that no matter what; one of them would climb the tall pine tree in the morning.

The next morning, Cream trotted out of her house, keeping an eye out for Ember. Truthfully, she felt bad, and wanted to apologize for the previous morning. Maybe even invite her to play. But she didn't see Ember anywhere.

She was the first kitten to the tree. She sat at the base, waiting for her friends, when she heard a voice from above her.

"Good morning," the voice said timidly. She looked up and saw Ember at the very top of the tree!

"Ember!" Cream gasped. "How did you get up there?"

Ember shrugged. "I climbed."

"But...but weren't you scared?" Cream couldn't believe how high up Ember was.

The orange and white kitten just shook her head. "I love to climb." Shyly, she climbed a few branches down, until she was just above Cream's head. "I could show you guys the easiest way, if you want?"

Gratefully, Cream nodded her head. "Thanks, Ember."

By the time Smoky, Rusty, and Dot arrived, Cream was already high in the tree with Ember. Ember then spent the rest of the day showing the other cats how to climb up the tree, and even jumping back and for between the branches.

When sunset came, all five kittens were perched on the highest branch, watching the sun drift below the trees.

"Thanks, Ember," Cream said again. "I'm sorry we didn't play with you at first."

"I'm sorry, too," Rusty said. "You're a really good climber. We should have let you play with us the first time."

"It's okay," Ember said, flicking her tail happily. "Maybe you guys could show me the best rocks to get moss from?"

"Of course!" Dot said happily. "Do you want to come down to the stream with us tomorrow?"

"Yes!" Ember purred.

The next day, Cream, Dot, Rusty, and Smoky showed Ember the best places to get moss from the rocks. The day after that, they showed her the bed of springy pine needles they used to jump up and down. Then, it was a trip to where the wild daffodils grew.

Cream started leaving her house every morning, picking up Ember next door before heading into the woods to meet their other friends. Soon enough, the kittens were going on adventures every day. And pretty quickly, Cream and her friends realized that five friends were way better than four.

STORY #2: SWAN POND

Swan Lake was a magical place, full of beautiful creatures, crystal blue waters, and towering trees. The swans of Swan Lake spent their days dancing, singing, and casting magical spells on the world around them. They would create pink bubbles that danced through the air, enchant frogs to make them speak, and turn fish silver. It truly was an amazing place.

Right next to Swan Lake sat Swan Pond.

Diamond had lived in Swan Pond her entire life. Unlike the swans in Swan Lake, the swans in Swan Pond had no magical powers. They spent their days swimming, catching fish, and waiting for the fishermen to throw chunks of bread off the dock into their waiting mouths.

"I hate Swan Pond!" Diamond would complain. "I want to live in Swan Lake and be magical!"

"Oh, Diamond," her mother would say, "You *are* magical. Just in a different way."

Whatever, Diamond would think, ruffling her feathers. *I don't want to be magical in a different way. I want to be magical like the swans on Swan Lake.*

One day, as Diamond was doing her usual glide across the pond, anxiously waiting for the fishermen to lumber down to the dock, she spotted a strange looking swan in the distance.

This swan was much bigger than Diamond, with feathers that sparkled just the faintest pink, and a shiny yellow beak. This swam looked different. This swan looked like…

Diamond gasped. This was one of the swans from Swan Lake! A *magical* swan!

She churned her legs as fast as she could, gliding towards this new and magnificent creature. As she got closer though, it was clear that something was wrong. This swan looked lost, its eyes were large and scared. When it saw Diamond coming, its face brightened.

"Hello!" the swan said, eyeing Diamond nervously. "I'm Veronica. My mother was teaching me how to fly today, and she told me to land in the lake. But I missed and landed here instead. Can you tell me where I am?"

Diamond was mesmerized by the sound of Veronica's voice, and the way rainbows seemed to dance around her. It took her a second to even realize Veronica had asked her a question.

"Oh," Diamond said, worried she was about to scare this swan away. "You're in Swan Pond."

"Oh no!" Veronica said, spinning in an anxious circle. "I'm supposed to be in *Swan Lake*. It'll take my mother forever to find me!"

"Why don't you just fly to Swan Lake?" Diamond asked, confused.

Veronica looked embarrassed. "Well…I can't really fly that well yet. I'm still learning."

"It's okay," said Diamond soothingly, beckoning Veronica closer with her wing. "I will stay with you until your mother finds you."

Veronica looked relieved. "Thank you." A faint gurgle came from her stomach. She looked away, seemingly more embarrassed than she had been a minute ago. "Sorry. I'm just hungry."

"No problem!" said Diamond brightly. "Let's go get something to eat!"

Diamond turned and glided back towards the dock, moving slowly so Veronica could follow her. By the time they reached the dock, the fishermen were there, unhooking tackle boxes and casting their thin fishing lines into the water.

"How do we get food from here?" Veronica asked, confused.

"Easy!" Diamond responded, surprised Veronica didn't know how. "We just get up close to the fishermen, and they'll give us bits of bread from their sandwiches. Are there no fishermen in Swan Lake?"

Veronica shook her head, eyeing the fishermen warily. "No. Usually we just cast a spell, and cupcakes and pies grow up out of the lily pads."

"Wow," Diamond said, amazed. She hoped the plain old bread the fishermen offered them wouldn't disappoint Veronica. Beckoning with her long neck, Diamond glided closer to the dock, zigzagging to avoid becoming tangled in the fishermen's line. She heard Veronica moving much slower behind her, clearly having trouble avoiding the gossamer lines.

She approached her favorite fisherman, a jolly fellow who had a big bushy beard and always wore a red cap. "Hello, princess," the fisherman chuckled fondly, reaching into his lunchbox. "I brought a whole loaf just for you today." He pulled out a fat white chunk of bread, freshly baked and smelling absolutely heavenly. "Thank goodness too, because it looks like you brought a friend." He smiled widely at Veronica, who ducked her head shyly.

Pulling off bits at a time, he fed the two swans the entire loaf. "Goodness!" Veronica exclaimed, chewing slowly. "This is the most delicious thing I've ever eaten!"

Diamond swelled with pride. She had actually impressed a *Swan Lake* swan!

For the rest of the day, Diamond showed Veronica around Swan Pond.

She was amazed at everything she saw. "These fish are so big!" she said as Diamond reached into the water and pulled a huge black catfish out, its tail spraying drops of water all over their faces. "And you can just catch it like that?"

"You swim so fast!" Veronica said later, as Diamond demonstrated how to make figure eights through the water. "We always just cast a spell to make ourselves move. And you can do it all by yourself!"

Her mother's voice echoed in Diamond's head. *You are magical. Just in a different way.*

When the sun was getting ready to set, Diamond and Veronica saw an enormous pink swan swooping down from the sky, squawking anxiously. "My mother!" Veronica exclaimed, churning her legs through the water like Diamond had shown her earlier. "Mama! Over here!"

Veronica's mother landed gracefully on the pond, turning her head towards the noise. "Oh, Veronica! There you are. I was worried sick."

"I'm okay!" Veronica said, nudging her beak into Diamond's feathers. "This is Diamond. She's been helping me all day!"

"Oh, thank you," the bigger swan said, turning to nudge Diamond's feathers as well. "You are simply magical, darling. You are always welcome in Swan Lake."

"Actually, mama," Veronica said nervously. "Maybe I could come to visit her in Swan Pond again? It's so much fun here."

"Of course," she purred back. "Now let's get you home."

Diamond watched the two swans begin to beat their wings, Veronica's mother giving her a little push so she shot into the sky first. Diamond smoothed her ruffled feathers, her heart so full of joy it felt like it might burst.

She glided back across the pond towards her mother, thinking all the while, *I guess I am magical after all.*

STORY #3: PRINCESS NINA

Princess Nina lived in a tall tower in the middle of a dense forest with her father, King Jordan. He presided over the surrounding kingdom with a fair but firm attitude, which was also how he parented his only daughter.

After Princess Nina's mother had died when she was two, King Jordan had become very protective of her. He only allowed her to leave the tower during the day, and demanded she is back in time for dinner. Because their tower was so far away from the surrounding villages, Nina had no friends, and very few things to do.

Luckily, however, Nina had a special talent.

She discovered it one day as she was wandering about the woods near the tower, picking juicy, plump berries to take home and make into a tart. Hearing branches break behind her, she spun on her heel, fearing a bear or a bobcat. However, it was just a deer. A lovely doe, with huge eyes and splotches of white on its coat.

"Oh," she said without thinking. "I'm sorry. You surprised me."

However, Nina was even more surprised when the deer began to speak back.

"It's okay," the deer replied. "Those berries smell very good, you know."

Her hands trembling, Nina stretched out one palm full of berries, towards the deer's twitching nose. "You can talk," she murmured, watching in awe as the deer began to snack on the fat, red fruit.

"Of course, I can," the deer replied, munching away. "The interesting part is that you can understand me."

From that day forward, Nina spent all of her free time in the woods, meeting birds and rabbits and chipmunks and deer, chatting with them about her day, about the forest, and about which trees had the juiciest berries or the softest leaves.

One day, she was involved in a fairly heated debate between two squirrels, which were each very convinced *their* tree was the best.

"The pine tree by the pond has the highest branches!" the first squirrel argued.

"That may be true," the second squirrel said back, "but the oak tree in the clearing gets the best sunlight for napping."

"Okay, friends, I know you're upset, but-" Suddenly, Nina stopped, casting her eyes towards the sky. It had suddenly gone from blue to violet to almost navy blue, a sure sign that the sun had set. "Oh no!" she gasped. "It's after sunset! I *must* get home!"

Bidding goodbye to the squirrels, Nina raced out of the clearing, heading towards what she thought was the tower.

However, after a moment, she stopped short. She didn't recognize the large, gnarled trees that suddenly surrounded her. And she couldn't see the stream that she usually followed to get home.

Was she lost? No, no, it couldn't be. Nina turned and raced desperately back in the other direction, but she couldn't see the stream there either. She ran through another copse of trees, but this one led her to a fearsome looking cave.

Defeated and frightened, Nina sat down at the mouth of the cave and began to cry. Suddenly, she felt a huge paw settle on her shoulder. She turned timidly, and screamed when she saw an enormous bear behind her.

"Don't be afraid, child," the bear said soothingly. "I've heard of you. You're the princess that speaks to animals."

Sniffling, Nina nodded.

"Are you lost?" the bear asked. Nina nodded again. "Ah. You live in the tower, right? Let me help you get home."

Gratefully, Nina rose to her feet, following behind the lumbering bear as they made their way through the woods, the bear breaking down branches to let Nina pass.

Finally, they reached the stream. Nina breathed a sigh of relief, but then realized that she wasn't sure which way to follow the stream in order to get back to the tower.

"This is where my help ends," the bear said. Nina started to panic again, but the bear nodded towards the hollow of a nearby tree. "Another friend will help you with the next leg of the journey."

An owl stuck its head out of the tree, cooing towards Nina. "Hello, princess. Let me help you get the rest of the way home."

Nina smiled, watching as the mottled bird sprang from its perch in the tree, its wings a shining beacon towards home. She had to run to keep up with the powerful bird, but she didn't mind. Gathering up her skirts, she jumped over tree roots and rocks, keeping her eyes on the owl the whole time.

The owl stopped at a massive oak tree, settling onto a branch. "This is as far as I go," the owl said, twitching its beak towards the ground. "Your old friend will make sure you reach the tower."

From behind the tree stepped the doe that Nina had first spoken to that day so long ago in the forest. "Princess," she said, dipping her head in greeting. "Let's get you back to the tower."

With one hand on the deer's flank, Nina allowed her to lead the way through the forest, until the darkness cleared and the stars became visible. Finally, with a cry of relief, Nina saw the tower, illuminated against the full moon.

"Oh!" she cried, throwing her arms around the deer's neck in a grateful embrace. "Thank you so much!"

The deer nuzzled her cheek. "Anything for a friend," the deer murmured back. "And remember, you are always braver than you think." With the second dip of her head, the doe retreated back into the forest.

Nina's father was so relieved to see her that he couldn't stay mad for long. The next day, Nina walked into her father's chambers, getting ready to tell him she was going into the forest for the day. However, at the very last minute, she changed her mind.

"Papa?" she said. "How would you like to come to the woods with me? There's something I'd like you to see."

STORY #4: THE MAKING OF PEARLS

The mermaids of the Emerald Sea were good at many things. They could swim well, speak to fish, and create beautiful tapestries out of seaweed. However, what they were best at was their most important task: making the beautiful pearls that went into the mouths of clams.

Every mermaid began to make their own pearls on their eleventh birthday. On Jade's eleventh birthday, she woke up early and swam around in circles in her cave, waking up her disgruntled parents.

"Today I learn to make pearls!" she told them excitedly.

"Yes, we know," her mother said in a tired voice. "Go back to sleep for a little while, please."

But Jade couldn't sleep. She tried to lie back down, but her body vibrated with excitement. *I'm going to be the best pearl maker in the sea.*

Jade and the other young mermaids joined their instructor, Miss Rosa, on the ocean floor. The older mermaid sat primly on a rock, while the rest of the mermaids gathered at her feet.

"Today, class," Miss Rosa said, sweeping up a ball of white sand in her hands, "we are going to learn to make pearls."

Jade tried to listen to Miss Rosa's instructions, but she was too excited to concentrate. She wanted to learn how to make pearls *now*.

After what seemed like forever, Miss Rosa told them it was time to start making their own. The young mermaids settled on the ocean floor, lounging comfortably as they began to pick up their own balls of sand and move them softly in their hands, slowly creating beautiful, shiny, pearls.

Jade began to collect her own ball of sand, but every time she got it formed, it would dissolve back into the ocean. How had Miss Rosa told them to get the balls of sand to stick? She couldn't remember. She hadn't been listening. She had been much too excited about making the pearls, but now she didn't know how.

The rest of the mermaids and finished their pearls and were excitedly showing them to each other, but Jade was still struggling to form her ball of sand. She felt a hand on her shoulder. "Jade?" Miss Rosa asked. "Do you need help?"

"No!" Jade cried, as the sand settled back down at her tail once more. "No, I-"

"Do you remember how what I showed you?"

By now, the rest of the mermaids were looking at Jade. She felt her cheeks flush. "Were you listening?" Miss Rosa asked gently.

Jade was now so embarrassed she couldn't even look at the instructor. Instead, she turned and fled the group, swimming as high as she could, towards the watery sun.

Jade's head broke the surface of the water, and she realized she had swum towards the beach. Sobbing now, she swam to the shore, laying down on the sand and letting the waves crash over her.

Why hadn't she listened? Now she would never learn how to make pearls the right way. Her dreams were crushed.

She cried for hours, watching as the salty water washed each tear away. She cried for such a long time that she finally had no tears left. Then, she just stared at the sand and the setting sun.

Suddenly, she heard a splash beside her, and turned to see another, older mermaid swim up on shore beside her. This mermaid had long red hair, with seaweed braided throughout. Her eyes were the same color as the aqua around them. She was the most beautiful mermaid Jade had ever seen.

Jade watched in amazement as this mermaid slowly collected a ball of sand, rolling it very carefully in the palms of her hands. A thin cloud of silver smoke rose around the mermaid's hands, and then suddenly, POOF!

The ball of sand that had been sitting in the mermaid's hand a moment ago had suddenly become a beautiful, shining pearl. Smiling softly, the mermaid turned her head towards Jade's.

"Hello," she said in a whispery voice, "I see you watching me."

"Sorry," Jade said, turning away. "I just…I just…I wanted to watch you make the pearls. So I could learn. But I'm still confused." She felt like she was going to cry again.

"Well," the mermaid said, "I could teach you, if you want."

So, for the rest of the day, the red-haired mermaid taught Jade how to properly make a pearl. At first, Jade still didn't understand, and she became frustrated.

"I'm still not doing it right," she said, feeling disappointment.

"Here." The mermaid held out of her hands. "Watch me one more time. Listen very carefully."

So, this time, Jade did.

She listened and watched and watched and listened as the mermaid showed her one more time how to make a pearl. When she was done she nodded at Jade, and then at the sand.

"Go ahead," she said.

Slowly, Jade picked up the ball of sand, and then began to rotate it in her hands. This time, instead of the sand breaking apart or floating away, it began to harden. Faster and faster Jade's hands moved, until suddenly, it wasn't sand anymore.

It was a pearl!

"I did it!" Jade cried. The mermaid smiled, and let out a light, tinkling laugh.

"Yes," she replied, slowly letting the waves wash her away. "You did."

Jade was excited to show off her pearl to Miss Rosa and her classmates.

"I'm very proud of you, Jade," Miss Rosa said, turning the pearl around in her long, spidery fingers. "It's very beautiful."

"Thank you," Jade said happily, "I had help. And…and…I listened."

Miss Rosa smiled broadly.

Jade's favorite place remained the shore, where the waves would crash over, and the sand was perfect and white for pearl making. Every time she went, she searched for the red-haired mermaid, but never saw her again.

Sometimes though, right when she finished a pearl, she would glance up, thinking she had heard something. It was always the same sound.

A light, tinkling laugh.

STORY #5 - LIGHTNING BUG COVE

Lightning Bug Cove was in the heart of Wish Woods, and was called Lighting Bug Cove for a reason.

Every night, just before the sun finally kissed the edge of the Earth and then sunk into its slumber, thousands of lightning bugs would swarm out of the trees. They would make elaborate formations, spin in circles, and zoom to the very tops of their leafy home, taking in the sunset.

People marveled over these lightning bugs; how could they possibly form such amazing shapes? How did they move so quickly?

Well, it was because these lightning bugs weren't actually lightning bugs at all.

They were forest nymphs.

If you looked really closely- probably closer than anyone really could fathom- you could see for yourself. Each one had a tiny green body, tiny green wings, and a bead of light directly in between their shoulder blades. And if you listened really hard, you may even hear one of them let out a tiny giggle.

Over time, word spread in the village about the hidden cove of Wish Woods. More and more people wanted to make the trek through the woods in order to get to Lightning Bug Cove, so they too could see the elaborate lightning bug shows every night.

The nymphs were absolutely delighted.

If you know anything about forest nymphs, you know that they simply *love* to put on a show. They are creatures that thrive on attention; there's nothing they enjoy more than performing for an audience.

Reya was one of the prettiest nymphs in the whole cove, and one of the best dancers too. Every night, she was the first one to start dancing, and was usually the last one to stop too.

"Look!" she would say every night, pointing her long, slender finger towards the opening of the trees. "There are people coming! Are you guys ready?"

Her friends Dina, Mina, and Trina nodded. The four of them loved to dance for people more than any of the other nymphs in the cove. Every day, they practiced in the hollow of the trees, and every night, they were the stars of the show.

The rest of the nymphs sat gathered in the branches, waiting for Reya, Dina, Mina, and Trina to get started. As much as fairies love putting on a show, they love to watch others dance even more. And every nymph knew that those four were the absolute best dancers that Lightning Bug Cove had ever seen.

Once the evening hikers had gathered in the corner of the trees, eagerly waiting for the show to start, Reya turned towards her three friends.

"Okay," she said, grinning to the three nymphs behind her. "Let's do this!"

Reya would always start first, fanning out her wings and dipping into a low bow. Then, she was off, spinning and dancing and soaring high above the onlookers' heads all the way down to the forest floor.

Next Dina would start to dance, and then Mina, and finally Trina. The four would move in perfect unison with each other and the songs of the nightingales that sat in the hollows with the fairies, providing a lovely evening song. Soon, all the nymphs had joined in, making the hollow dance with dazzling light.

On this night however, something a little different happened. When Reya went to do her signature finishing move- a sweep almost to the ground and then a quick shot all the way up the tree- she went a little too fast, and hit the ground hard instead.

All the nymphs stopped and gasped. After a second, Reya pulled herself up, her wings slightly bent and her crown of daisies askew. Instead of finishing off the show, Reye slunk into the tree hollow silently.

After the sun was set and all the people had gone home for the evening, Dina, Mina, and Trina snuck into the knot in the tree where Reya sat curled on her side, tears streaming down her face.

"It's okay," Trina said gently, reaching down to hug her friend.

"It happens," Dina said, stroking Reya's bent wings.

"No one even noticed," Mina assured her.

But Reya didn't listen. All she could think about was how she had messed up the show. How would she ever be able to dance again?

For days, Reya sat in the hollow instead of dancing. While the other three nymphs put on a good opening act, it just wasn't the same without Reya leading the way.

"We have to make her feel better," Dina said.

"But how?" Mina asked, her brow furrowing in worry.

"Maybe if we unbend her wings, and get her a fresh daisy crown, she'll feel better," Trina suggested.

So, Mina went off in search of the plumpest daisies for a new crown. Dina and Trina flew into Reya's tree hollow; she still sat sadly on her tiny bark bed.

"Hey guys," she said glumly when she saw her friends approaching.

"Hey, Reya," the two said. "We're here to unbend your wings."

Without waiting for an answer, the two went to work on her shiny wings, slowly and carefully unbending each fold and smoothing them out until they looked good as new. Just as they were finishing up, Mina flew in holding the most beautiful daisy crown any of them had ever seen.

"Look, Reya," Mina said softly, placing the crown onto Reya's tiny head.

Reya looked into her raindrop mirror, marveling at her shiny, unbent wings and lovely crown. "Oh," she breathed, turning to each one of her friends. "It's beautiful. Thank you all."

Her three friends beamed. "Now," Trina said, "are you ready to dance?"

That night, Reya put on the most amazing show any of the nymphs in Lightning Bug Cove had ever seen. She spun, zigzagged, and ended the night with her signature move. The onlookers clapped and whistled when she was finished.

After the sunset, the four nymphs sat huddled on Reya's bed, brushing each other's hair.

"Thanks, guys," Reya said gratefully, smiling at her friends. "I guess I should have done that myself days ago."

Her three friends just shrugged. "Maybe," Dina said, "but after all, what are friends for?"

STORY #6— ANNA'S GARDEN

Anna lived at the edge of town, in a tiny, ramshackle house filled with odds and ends. Outside her home lay a shed, a broom, a cauldron, and the most beautiful flower garden you had seen.

Sometimes, when you would walk by Anna's old house, you may think you heard voices. Whispers, maybe. Or giggles.

That's because Anna wasn't just any old woman. She was a witch.

And the garden wasn't just any old garden. It was an *enchanted* garden.

Every morning, Anna woke up early and mixed up a special brew for all of her flowers.

"Good morning," she would say to each one, pouring the elixir out of her special watering can.

"Good morning," each flower would say back after drinking the potion.

The flowers were all very happy in their garden. The soil was rich, the ground was healthy, and the potions Anna brewed made them grow tall and strong.

Anna loved all of her flowers, but she had to admit that the roses were her absolute favorite. They grew in a variety of colors: pink, red, and white. They were soft to the touch, with perfectly sharp barbs to keep away pests. Each time she watered her garden, she would give them a little extra attention.

"Hello, my loves," she would coo, marveling over each one's beautiful petals and strong, green stalks.

One day, as she was admiring her roses, she noticed that a new rose was sprouting from the bottom of her favorite rose bush, which she called Clara.

"Well hello, little one," she purred, reaching out to stroke the baby rose's head.

"Oh, you've noticed my baby," Clara said proudly, shaking her petals in delight.

"So I have," Anna replied. "It may be small now, but one day it will go big and strong like you, Clara."

"So it will," Clara said. "As long as it gets plenty of your potion."

So Anna continued to water the roses every day, paying special attention to the baby rose.

However, even after a couple of weeks, the rose still hadn't grown any bigger.

"Why aren't I getting bigger, Mama?" the baby rose asked, pouting.

"Worry not, my little petal," Clara cooed to her baby, leaning down to look at its tiny pink petals. "Some roses just take a little longer to grow than others, that's all."

"Why aren't I getting bigger, Anna?" the baby rose repeated to the witch when she came outside for her daily watering.

"It's okay," Anna assured the baby rose, sprinkling her all over with her special brew. "Some things just take time, my love."

Months passed, and still, the rose barely got any bigger. One day, as Anna was watering her flowers, she remembered an old adage she had learned at her Witches Academy.

The same thing doesn't work for every witch, the Head Witch had told them, *certain spells may not work for certain people.*

"Hmmm," Anna said out loud. "Maybe I need to try something a little different."

When she went back inside, Anna began to brew a fresh potion. Instead of adding ginger root, she added St. John's Wart. And instead of black coffee, she added daisy tea.

"Let's see how this works!" Anna said, pouring her concoction into her watering can.

She headed back outside to where the little rose sat eagerly waiting.

"Okay," she told the baby rose, "Let's see if this does the trick."

She poured the potion over the baby rose, who fluttered its petals with excitement.

"Now we wait," Clara told the baby gently.

A week passed, but still the rose hadn't gotten any bigger.

"I'm never going to grow big and tall like you," the rose said sadly to Clara, letting its petals wilt towards the ground.

"Nonsense," Anna declared. "I'll figure it out."

This time, she added chamomile tea, milk, and lemon shavings. Pouring the mixture over the baby rose, she said, "Let's try this now, dear."

Still, however, the baby rose did not grow.

By this point the baby rose began to cry. It wanted too badly to grow big and tall like its mother, but it didn't seem like that was ever going to happen.

Clara soothed the rose, stretching out her thorns so they gently scratched the baby rose's stalk. "It's okay, my love."

"Don't worry," Anna assured the rose, squatting down to pat the baby's tiny petals. "The next one will work, I promise."

"What am I doing wrong?" Anna asked as she walked around her kitchen, searching for mixtures she hadn't tried yet. She opened a cabinet full of poultices, but they didn't look like they would help.

Frustrated, Anna slammed the cabinet door shut. Suddenly, she heard a faint tinkle. She looked down at her feet to see a tiny glass vial, full of a strange, silver powder.

She picked it up, twirling it in her fingers, as a memory of her own mother popped loose in her mind. *Having a hard time growing, are we?* Her mother said to her garden, pouring the powder over the flowers. *This powder is made of pure love. It helps even the tiniest flower grow big and strong.*

"That's it!" Anna cried, running outside with the vial in hand.

The baby rose was huddled next to Clara; its petals drooped in sadness.

"Don't be said, dear," Anna soothed the rose. "I think I have something that will finally help."

Uncorking the vial, she poured the love all over the baby rose. The rose turned its face to the sky, drinking in every last bit.

"Okay," Anna said the rose. "Now we wait."

A week later, Anna came outside with her watering can. She lugged it over to the garden.

"Good morning, flowers," she sang.

"Good morning, Anna," the flowers replied, as she began her daily ritual.

"Good morning, Anna," said a small voice, and she turned to the end of the garden.

There, next to Clara, was the baby rose, except it wasn't a baby anymore. It was tall and strong, with large, velvety petals and a thick green stalk.

"Look at you!" Anna marveled, as the baby rose fluttered its petals happily.

"Look at me," the rose repeated happily, stretching towards the sky. "All I needed was a little extra love!"

STORY #7— THUNDER TO THE RESCUE

Thunder was born on a stormy day in a small hollow in the forest. His mother, Tuka, told him stories about it all the time, especially now that they had left the hollow and were headed towards the north, where their new home lay.

"Did it storm all night, Mama?" Thunder asked excitedly, bounding ahead of his mother. He was still a small bear, with dark brown fur like Tuka's, but his mother assured him that one day he would grow big and strong just like her.

"It did, little bear," Tuka said, plodding along. They had been walking for what seemed like ages, but Tuka told Thunder it had actually only been three days. Thunder was so excited when the mountains began to appear, stretching towards the horizon like a line of sharp, jagged teeth.

"We follow the mountains," Tuka told him, chuckling under her breath as he made his way through the flowers. "But slow down, or you'll tire yourself out!"

"Okay, Mama," Thunder said, but he didn't want to slow down. It took everything he had to slow his steps so they matched his mother's pace. "I'm trying."

"I know you are, baby bear," she responded. "Don't worry, we'll get there."

The next day, Tuka showed Thunder how to catch fish. "Like this, baby bear," she said, dunking her enormous head in the water. After a second, she popped back up, her mouth clamped around an enormous, fat salmon.

Thunder tried, but every time he did, the fish slid right out of his mouth. "I can't do it!" he said with disappointment, flopping himself down onto the ground.

"You can," Tuka said gently. "You just need to keep trying."

But no matter how hard Thunder tried, he couldn't manage to catch a fish.

"It's okay," Tuka told him. "You're a smart little bear. You'll figure it out. We'll try again later."

The next day, they arrived at the mouth of a cave. It yawned open, revealing and dark and cozy sleeping space. In front of it, however, lay a tumble of large gray rocks. "This is where we will sleep overnight," Tuka told Thunder, flicking her nose towards the cave. "But we have to move these rocks out of the way first."

Tuka began to move the rocks from the mouth of the cave, using her powerful shoulder to shove each one away. Thunder tried to copy her, but he was just too small. Every time he shoved up against a boulder, it stayed exactly where it was.

"I can't do it!" Thunder said, hanging his head.

"You're just a little too small," Tuka said, patting him on the head with her enormous paw. "When you're big like me, you'll be able to do it, don't worry."

But Thunder didn't want to wait; he wanted to be able to do it *now*. He felt like he wasn't helping his mother at all.

The next day, they walked until the sun reached high in the sky, and Thunder told his mother he was hungry.

"Okay," Tuka said. "Let's climb a tree and get you some berries."

"Yummy!" Thunder said, gazing up at the tree. The berries, however, looked pretty high up.

"Watch me first," Tuka said, gripping the tree with her large arms. Slowly, she began to shimmy up, until she had reached a patch of fat red berries. She plucked a cluster of them, and then slid back down. "Now you try," she said through her mouthful.

Thunder tried, but he just couldn't get himself up the tree high enough. Every time he would think he was almost there, he slid right back down.

"I can't do it," Thunder said miserably. He felt like it was all he was saying these days.

"You just need to get a little bigger," Tuka soothed. "One day, you'll be able to do everything I do."

Thunder just eyed his mother. At this point, he wasn't so sure that was the truth.

That night, they slept in a large fort Tuka had built from tree branches. Once again, Thunder had tried to help, but just couldn't figure out how.

Instead, he sat curled in a ball next to his sleeping mother, feeling sad. How was he supposed to grow big and strong when he couldn't seem to do anything that she could?

As he was finally dozing off, he heard a sudden noise outside. It sounded a little bit like a hiss, and a little bit like a snarl. It sounded…it sounded like something that might try to hurt them!

Sticking his head out of the fort, he saw that a pack of wolves had surrounded their sleeping place, and they were pacing and snarling, clearly getting ready to attack. How was his mother supposed to fight them all off?

Maybe I can help, Thunder thought. But how could he help fight off the wolves when he could even build or climb or fish? His mother's voice echoed in his head. *You're a smart little bear.*

Looking up, he saw a huge branch dangling down over the wolves, in danger of falling at any moment. Without thinking twice, Thunder launched himself up out of the fort, grabbing onto the branch and swinging it back and forth with all his might.

The wolves began to chuckle. Who knew dinner would be this easy? But just as one of the wolves reached its paw up to swat Thunder down, the branch snapped, crashing down onto the wolves with a powerful *THUMP*.

The wolves, startled, immediately fled. Thunder lay in a heap, dizzy, as his mother awoke and rushed over to him.

"Thunder!" she gasped. "Are you okay?"

"Yes, mama," Thunder replied, getting to his feet. "I scared away the wolves!"

His mother's eyes grew wide. "You *did*?"

"I did! The tree branch scared them!" Thunder's chest swelled with pride.

"Thank you for all your help," his mother said gratefully.

I did it, thought Thunder. *I finally helped.*

"My brave, brave little bear," his mother cooed, gathering him tight in her arms. "What in the world would I do without you?"

"I don't know, Mama," Thunder said, and fell asleep with a big smile on his face.

STORY #8— A TALE OF TWO PRINCES

Once, in a kingdom far away, there lived two young princes. One of the princes had been born to the Queen and King. However, after the Queen died, the King remarried. His new wife had beautiful white wings that stretched towards the sky, and when the second prince was born, he had enormous white wings as well.

The younger prince loved his wings. He would spend hours grooming his glossy white feathers, and even more hours gazing at them in the mirror, admiring their beauty.

The older prince loved his brother's wings and wished desperately he had been born with them as well. What he wished even more, though, was that his younger brother would include him in his adventures.

"Sorry," the younger prince would shrug when his older brother would ask to join him on a journey. "You'd have to fly, too, and you can't." With that, he would soar out of their open bedroom window and into the valley below.

"Maybe one day we could walk through the valley on foot?" the older prince would ask his brother hopefully.

His brother, however, would usually just shrug. "Why in the world would I walk when I could fly?"

"Okay," the older prince would say back, disappointed.

Because of this, the older prince spent a lot of his time alone. He was very lonely. He tried to explore the countryside on his own, but would always think to himself, *I wish I had a friend.*

One day, the younger prince announced to his older brother this his plan for the day was to fly all the way to the sun.

"All the way to the sun?" the older prince asked doubtfully. "Are you sure that's a good idea?"

"Of course, it is," the younger prince replied snottily. "Anyway, how would you know? You don't even have any wings."

That's true, the older prince thought. *But how I wish I did.*

The younger prince spent all morning telling everyone in the castle his plan. By the afternoon, a huge crowd had gathered in the square below, ready to watch the young prince with wings fly all the way to the sun.

The older prince sat in his bedroom, watching his younger brother groom his wings in preparation to take flight.

"I wish I could come with you," the older prince said glumly.

The young prince laughed. "How could you, when you don't have any wings?" With that, he turned towards the window, addressing the crowd below. "Who would like to see me fly towards the sun?"

The crowd roared with excitement. "Wish me luck, brother," the younger prince crowed, and flew from the window in one large leap.

"Good luck," the older prince whispered, but his brother was already gone. The crowd watched in amazement as the younger prince soared and swooped, finally speeding as fast as he could towards the sun.

The older prince watched, but couldn't shake the feeling that something was wrong. He couldn't put his finger on it, but the feeling caused him to move his feet all the way down to the bottom of the castle, out the door, and into the woods, watching his younger brother all the while.

By now, the younger prince was barely a speck in the sky. The older prince craned his head back as far as he could see, his eyes on his brother. The closer he got to the sun, however, the slower his brother seemed to move. Suddenly, his brother stopped completely.

Just then, the older prince finally realized what was wrong.

The sun, he thought, watching in horror as his brother began to writhe about in the sky. *The sun is going to burn his wings.*

He could still hear the shouts of the crowd behind him, convinced that the younger prince was simply performing some kind of dance. Suddenly, however, the crowd fell silent, and then the gasps began.

"He's going to fall!" someone shouted, and as soon as they said that, the younger prince began to career out of the sky.

The older prince began running as fast as he could towards the spot where his brother was falling. *I'll never make it in time*, he thought desperately. He began to move his legs faster, and finally, began to jump. Every time he took a big leap, it sort of felt like he was flying, too.

He made it to the clearing just as his brother was plummeting down. He caught him in his arms, falling to the ground himself. The younger prince's wings were burned, black creeping along where the white used to be. "My wings," the younger prince whispered. "They're ruined." Tears began to leak out of his eyes.

"I'm sorry," his older brother replied, cradling him like he was a baby again.

"You saved me," he said back, looking at his brother with wonder. "You saved me, even after how I've treated you."

"Of course," said the older prince, shrugging. "We're still brothers."

The older prince carried his younger brother all the way back to the castle, letting him rest his head on his chest the entire way there. When they finally got back, the younger prince was sent to the infirmary, where he had to rest for weeks on end.

Every day, his older brother went to visit him, and over time, the two became something they had never been before: friends. Finally, the day came when the younger prince was allowed to leave the infirmary. His wings were gone, clipped neatly at his shoulders. When he walked out, his older brother was waiting for him. "Brother," the younger prince said warmly, embracing the older prince. "What shall we do, now that I'm healed?"

"Well," the older prince replied hesitantly. "I was thinking we could take a walk through the countryside?" He held his breath, waiting to see how his younger brother would respond.

"That," the younger prince said, a slow smile stretching across his face, "sounds like a wonderful idea."

STORY #9— MARIA AND THE WOLVES

Princess Maria had a happy life with her parents, the King and Queen. One day, however, her mother fell ill, and simply couldn't seem to get any better. Maria and her father did everything they could to help her, but after a few weeks, the unimaginable happened.

The Queen died.

Her father was devastated. He took to his chambers for months, only leaving to eat. When he finally started coming out more often, Maria learned the reason why.

Maria's new stepmother did not like her. That much, Maria was sure. Even on their wedding day, when her father insisted that she come up to the altar, her stepmother glared at her. And Maria understood why. She heard the whispers everywhere. *Princess Maria*, they would say, *is more beautiful than the Queen herself.*

Her stepmother wanted to be the most beautiful woman in all of the land. And she would stop at nothing to get it.

"Come here, child," she would say, beckoning Maria closer to one long, red fingernail. But when Maria got close, she would see the knife the Queen had hidden behind her back. And she would run away.

When her stepmother would serve Maria dinner, she wouldn't touch any of it. She knew that her stepmother had filled the food with powders and poisons that would make Maria drop dead.

While Maria thought the worst thing that could happen was the Queen dying, she had been wrong. One day, the King died too.

Now, Maria was left alone with her evil stepmother, who she knew would never rest until she was the fairest woman in the land.

So, Maria decided to run away.

She left in the dead of night, taking nothing with her except a locket containing a picture of her mother. "Help me, mother," she whispered, holding the locket close as she ventured out into the woods.

The forest was dark and frightening. Maria had no idea where she was going, and no idea how she was supposed to find a place where she could eat and rest.

She walked until she couldn't anymore, and finally lay down outside the mouth of a cave and began to cry.

"Don't cry," came a small voice from behind her. She jerked upright, turning to see seven small wolf cubs watching her curiously.

She did the first thing she could think to do, which was scream.

"Don't be frightened," another cub said, coming closer to Maria. "We mean you no harm. Would you like to join us in our cave?"

Maria was frightened, but she didn't know what other options she had. So, nervously, she followed the wolves into their cave.

Before long, she considered all seven of the wolves her friends. She would keep the cave clean while they would go out and hunt, and at night she would roast their catch over the fire and they would trade stories.

Maria lived happily with the wolves for two years. Her stepmother, believing her dead, declared herself the fairest in the land, something that Maria didn't mind one bit. She didn't care if she was beautiful or not. She only cared about having good company, which she found with her seven wolves.

Every night, she would thank the wolves. "Thank you for taking me in," she would say gratefully while she roasted a freshly caught rabbit over the fire.

"No, Maria," the wolves would reply, "Thank *you*."

Over time, however, Maria began to feel a little lonely. She loved the wolves, of course, but she missed human companionship. And she was nearing the age where it was time to be married.

One night, she glumly told the seven wolves how she was feeling. After she fell asleep, the wolves made a pact to find Maria a husband.

The next day, Maria headed into the forest in search of elderberries to make a poultice. She found a bush full of ripe purple berries and was under the impression that they were the elderberries she was seeking.

Popping a handful in her mouth, she continued her daily gathering.

However, by the time she got back to the cave, she was feeling weak and sluggish. The wolves were waiting for her outside, but as she walked up to them, she suddenly fell to the ground.

"The berries!" one of the wolves gasped, jerking his nose towards the berries rolling from Maria's basket. "They're sleeping beads! Oh, dear."

The wolves hauled Maria into the cave, where they placed her onto the bed. They licked and nudged her in an attempt to wake her up, but to no avail.

"It won't work," one of the wolves said miserably. "She can only wake from sleeping beads if she is kissed by someone who truly understands her."

Luckily, the wolves had been scheming to find Maria a husband. Every day, a different prince would come from a faraway land and try their luck with waking Maria up. But it didn't work. The princes were all stuffy and smug, which wasn't like Maria at all. So far, none of her suitors truly understood her.

Finally, one day, an outdoorsman arrived at the mouth of the cave. He was not a prince; in fact, he would be considered a peasant. He was, however, brave, adventurous, kind, and most of all, humble.

Just like Maria.

The outdoorsman entered the cave, the wolves trailing behind. When he got to Maria's bedside, he bent down beside her.

"Nice to meet you, Maria," he said formally. Reaching over, he planted a friendly kiss on her cheeks.

Instantly, Maria's eyes shot open. The outdoorsman stumbled back, startled.

"Hello," he said gently. "I'm Andre."

"Hello," Maria said back, blushing. How could that be? She barely knew this man. "I'm Maria."

"Well, Maria," Andre said, a blush of his own creeping up towards his cheeks. "I heard you live with wolves. That makes you very…"

Maria held her breath.

"Brave. And strong. And courageous. And," he said, leaning down to plant another kiss on her cheek. "The exact kind of person I want to share my life with."

STORY #10— LOLA'S DRAWINGS

There was nothing Lola loved to do more than draw. Every day after school, she would sit at her desk and draw pictures of dragons, and unicorns, and enormous tigers baring their sharp teeth.

Her parents bought her stacks of paper, crayons, markers, and colored pencils, but every week like clockwork she asked for more.

"At least she likes to draw," her father would say, shrugging his shoulders.

"Could be worse," her mother agreed.

One day, Lola got home from school, and began to draw as she normally did. But as Lola was drawing a horse, she noticed something. Where she had colored in the horse's dark brown flank was beginning to move.

She blinked a couple of times, shaking her head. *Was she seeing thing*s*?* She continued to draw, keeping an eye on the horse as she did so.

Suddenly, the horse moved again. Lola gasped, dropping her crayon onto the ground. The horse wiggled again, then turned the head Lola had just drawn to look at her.

Neeeeiiiiiggghhhhh. Lola pushed away from the desk entirely. *Now she was hearing things?* As she stared at the horse in amazement, it slowly detached itself from the paper and leapt up into her bedroom.

"Wow," Lola whispered softly, reaching her hand out to pet the stallion's velvety nose. "Are you real?"

The horse just whinnied in response, tossing its head back and forth as if telling her; *Of course, I'm real.*

"No way," Lola said, louder this time. She began to get giddy with excitement. "No way!"

Lola didn't know what to do with the horse in her bedroom. What was she supposed to tell her parents? So, before she went to bed, she led the horse into her bathroom, filling up the sink with water so it could drink.

"Stay here," she told the horse anxiously. "I'll figure out what to do with you in the morning."

The next morning when she woke up, the first thing she did was a race to the bathroom and yank the door open. To her surprise, the horse was gone. She backtracked back to her desk, where the piece of formerly blank paper lay. Now, the horse was back on the paper, just in a different position than it had been in when she drew it.

"Wow," she whispered. "This is *so cool!*"

For the next week, all Lola did after school was a draw. She even drew all day on the weekends, forgetting about play dates and the swimming pool and the park and all the other things she usually did on the weekend.

"She does love to draw," said her father, shrugging.

"Nothing wrong with that," her mother agreed.

Lola drew birds and bees and cats and dogs and deer. She drew unicorns and frogs and fairies and huge, cheesy pizzas with shiny pepperonis. Every single thing she drew jumped off the page, appearing in her room as if it were real.

She took a bite of the pizza, watching in amazement as the cheese stretched from the slice into her open mouth. It tasted like heaven.

She drew big, fluffy white cats with blue eyes, and tiny chipmunks that scampered up and down her bedposts. She spent an hour drawing an ornate stained glass window, lifting it carefully off of the paper so it wouldn't break.

Lola was giddy with excitement. She could draw anything!

She drew an enormous crown and a huge diamond necklace. She gave herself matching bracelets and earrings. But they were too heavy on her wrists and earlobes, so she reluctantly took them off.

Pretty soon, Lola was drawing faster than she ever had before. She just couldn't stop! Every time she drew one thing, her mind immediately thought of something else she could draw.

She began drawing so fast that she was only spending a few seconds on each drawing before moving on to the next. Her brain was moving way faster than her hands could manage!

However, once she began drawing faster, she began to notice a problem. Her drawings were starting to look a little weird. The spider she had drawn had spun a web in the corner of her bedroom, but it only had six legs. The flock of flamingos were pale yellow, not pink, and their beaks were lopsided. The ponies she had meant to draw pale purple were actually just a dirty white color instead, and they were completely missing their manes!

She looked around her bedroom, beginning to panic. All of her drawings were messed up now! She had never messed up her drawings before.

A fairy flew towards her, but its wings were tiny and misshapen. She remembered drawing them, her mind already on the enormous turtle she wanted to draw next.

She cupped the fairy in her hands, stroking its head gently. "I'm sorry," she whispered. "I've been going too fast. I've been so focused on what to draw next I'm not paying attention to what I'm drawing *now*."

Laying the fairy on her desk, she covered it with a tiny Kleenex so it could take a nap. "I'll fix this," she promised.

The next morning, Lola woke up early. She spent all day fixing her drawings; adding extra legs to her spider, coloring in her flamingos, adding manes to her ponies. She slowly re-drew her fairy's wings, making sure that they were the right size this time.

That night, when she went to bed, she smiled at all of her creations, settling down for their own slumber. "I'm sorry, everyone," she said, "It won't happen again." When she woke up, all of her drawings had returned to their papers. What should she draw today?

Carefully, she grabbed a fresh piece of paper and a thick black crayon. She slowly drew an outline, and then colored it in with the brightest red crayon she could find in the box. It took her a long time, but all good things did.

When she was done, a perfect, shiny red apple sat on her desk. Smiling, Lola took a bite.

DISCLAIMER

This book contains opinions and ideas of the author and is meant to teach the reader informative and helpful knowledge while due care should be taken by the user in the application of the information provided. The instructions and strategies are possibly not right for every reader and there is no guarantee that they work for everyone. Using this book and implementing the information/recipes therein contained is explicitly your own responsibility and risk. This work with all its contents, does not guarantee correctness, completion, quality or correctness of the provided information. Misinformation or misprints cannot be completely eliminated.